Cyborgs Book 3:

The Greatest Hackers in the Universe

Ali Noel Vyain

Elsewhere

eISBN: 9781005762995

print ISBN: 9798201213664

1st edition printing

alinoelvyain.wordpress.com

Also By Ali Noel Vyain

The Colonies of Earth Series
The Colonies of Earth (Eris): Different
The Colonies of Earth (Venus): In Men's Shadows
The Colonies of Earth Series: Tales From Mars
The Colonies of Earth: The Colonies Will Be Independent
The Colonies of Earth: (Orcus): The Amazons Rise Up
The Colonies of Earth (Pluto): First Time
The Colonies of Earth (Saturn & Titan): Praying for Death
The Colonies of Earth (Mercury): This Strange, Wild Land
The Colonies of Earth (The Moon): The Crossroads
The Colonies of Earth (Triton): The Mistress
The Colonies of Earth (Neptune): The Plantation Owner
The Colonies of Earth (Ceres): The Vampire's Girlfriend
The Colonies of Earth (Titania): Vampire Struggles
The Colonies of Earth (Haumea): Aftermath
The Colonies of Earth: Box Set

The Starlover Series
Book 1: Project Earth
Book 2: Uncle & Niece
Book 3: Traveling Teenager
Book 4: Cassandra the Red Tiger
The Starlover Series Box Set

The Violet Series

The Guardian Series

Book 9: The Dragons of the Four Realms
Book 10: Faedin Returns
Book 11: Paradise Regained
Book 12: Grand Rock Junction
Book 13: Crime of Love
Book 14: The Lost Glory of Elsewhere
The Guardian Series Box Set

The White Lion Unicorn Series
Book 1: A Colony of Tiny Nekos
Book 2: The Cats of Elsewhere
Book 3: Her Name is Elsewhere
Book 4: The Death of Elsewhere
Book 5: The Black Unicorn and the Winged Lion
Book 6: The Rebirth of Elsewhere
Book 7: The Childhood of Elsewhere
Book 8: The Adolescence of Elsewhere
Book 9: Elsewhere City & Spirit
The White Lion Unicorn Series Box Set

The Titanium Mysteries
Book 1: What Is She Doing Here?
Book 2: Werewolves
Book 3: Zombies
Book 4: Vampires

Sir Socks Le Chat

Poetry

Discounted
Drugs
Falling in Love
The 7 Deadly Sins of Xmas
Fragments
Unrealistic Expectations
Deviation
Changling

Non-Fiction Books
Publishing 101: How to Publish Books While Spending Little to No Money at All
How to Build an Ebook Using XHTML & Calibre
Hyperspace
Various Articles

Contents

Chapter 1 Mastermind

He smiled to himself. He had built his own empire from the money he had inherited. It had taken him years and he didn't care. Things were wonderful so far. He thought perhaps it was time to get married to keep the money and family legacy together. He knew who he would ask even though he never knew her well. What he did know was that she was into play rather than any kind of work.

He spent time selecting a nice suit and got dressed. He checked himself in the mirror and smoothed his hair. He smiled at his reflection. He was ready to meet her and her twin brother. He took his private transport and soon found himself at the Rosendroff Estate. Technically as a Rosendroff himself, he didn't need any permission to show up unannounced.

He was let in by the robots and who quickly introduced him to both Renée and Phillipe Rosendroff.

"I present to you, Harold Rosendroff."

Both Phillipe and Renée blinked.

Phillipe spoke first, "Hello, cousin. What brings you here today?"

Harold bowed. "I came to ask for Renée's hand in marriage. I'm sure an alliance between us will keep the family legacy going strong."

Renée frowned. "You're an old man. I deserve someone

young. You probably couldn't keep up with me in bed."

Harold gasped. "I would do my best to satisfy you."

Renée scoffed. "It's so obvious that you couldn't. You're already bald and what hair you have left is white. And just look at your wrinkles!"

Harold sighed. "Is that your answer? Amazing. You're quite spoiled, Renée."

Renée continued, "No good for me. I prefer young men who can go all night long. I know I'm just getting started and should have lots of years to come in which I will be able to enjoy myself thoroughly. But not with an old man such as yourself."

Harold said, "Good day, cousins." He turned and left the estate never to return to it.

Harold was having a meeting with Edward and Lyndsy Edmunch. He called them in to learn more about the research they were doing.

Harold started the meeting. "I see you two are researching androids. What progress have you made so far?"

Edward answered, "We have a few robots so far and they do much of the menial work. We're currently trying to figure out how to create a butler android."

Lyndsy smiled. "We have him designed as far as how he will look. We are having a bit of trouble setting up his brain. However, we are doing our best to base it on how our brains work."

Harold nodded. "I have looked over your notes and reports so far and everything looks good to me. I would like to fund your research and help you get better equipment. I realize what you've been using is quite good, but I know there is better out there to help you understand how brains work."

Lyndsy asked, "What do you want in return?"

Harold smiled. "You can make me a robot butler too. Just don't make him look like yours. I would prefer someone a bit older."

Edward smiled. "Perhaps more like you?"

Harold nodded. "That would be great. Let me know as soon as you've discovered how to design the brain."

Edward and Lyndsy looked at each other and nodded.

Edward said, "Then we accept those terms."

Harold read the latest report from the Edmunch couple. He smiled. They had finally figured out how to design android brains. They had also designed the look of Harold's butler and he liked the result. He approved the design for his butler.

He stood up from his desk and turned to look out the window. He was looking forward to having an android butler. His current butler was about to retire and Harold wasn't able to find a replacement. His current butler had a few suggestions, but none had panned out. Harold wasn't about to throw out his current butler out of the house. They had an arrangement that he could stay on and train the android. That way the current butler would be able to retire and enjoy the rest of his life.

An alarm blared. Harold turned and pressed a button on his desk. "What is happening?"

"Sir, someone is hacking into our system."

"Where are they?"

"Apparently the breach is happening within the building. Someone down here."

"I'm on my way." Harold ran to the elevator and got to the floor where the computer was getting hacked.

He stepped out of the elevator to see some of his security personnel restraining a young man who appeared to be close to Renée and Phillipe's age.

Harold frowned at the kid. "How bad is the breach?"

"He was about to wipe the whole memory of our entire system and take it with him."

"Really. That's quite a feat before the alarm went off." Harold stepped closer to the kid. "What's your name?"

"Douglas Younon."

"Have you done this before?"

"Well, not on this scale. Just some minor things at school before they kicked me out."

"I see." Harold sighed and walked about the boy. The middle aged man had to assessed the boy. "So, you're interested in my company and its work?"

Douglas Younon nodded.

Harold growled softly. He stopped and faced the kid. "I'm willing to make a deal with you and let you go free if you do a job for me."

"What kind of job?"

"I need some information from one of my competitors. If you can get into their company headquarters and steal the information as you were in the middle of doing here, I can let you go. How does that sound?"

"Sounds good to me. I'll be quick about it."

"Good. Steal the files and erase their files on their computers. Once I get those files from you, I will let you go."

"And if I do a good job, will you ask me to do more jobs like that in the future?"

Harold smiled. "I just might."

Douglas Younon proved himself valuable and Harold did hire him to do other jobs over the years. Harold even did one sneaky thing Douglas was never aware of. Harold made sure Douglas would meet Renée. Harold was well aware of how attractive Renée and Phillipe Rosendroff were and of their parties. Harold smiled knowing what would happened between Douglas and Renée.

Harold played a long game. He wasn't into quick revenge. Just used a long term strategy which proved to keep him in business for quite a long time. Over the years, he continued to use Douglas to thwart Phillipe in learning about androids.

One thing made Harold frowned. Renée had a young child named Lynda and Renée had married their cousin George Rosendroff. Harold knew Edward and Lyndsy had a young boy by this time named Augustus. It wasn't the children that had made Harold frowned. It was the fact that Edward and Lyndsy were found murdered and their son was now missing from their estate.

Harold sighed. He liked Edward and Lyndsy. He hadn't met their son, but it didn't matter. Harold knew he had put something into motion and was sure Lynda was Douglas' biological daughter. Knowing where Augustus was would become important and Harold did what he could to find the boy to keep him away from Phillipe Rosendroff.

It was the only thing Harold could do to honour the memory of Edward and Lyndsy Edmunch and their work. Harold would be an old man before he learned what had become of both Lynda Rosendroff and Augustus Edmunch. Harold was a very patient man. He was willing to wait until the end of his life if necessary.

At least the android butler Edward and Lyndsy Edmunch made him worked out well. Harold was pleased to discover the butler was fairly well trained before his old butler met the android. That just made things goes much smoother as the human butler retired and enjoyed the rest of his life with an android learning the ways of Harold Edmunch and how to run his household.

Harold appreciated the butler and was glad he was able to let Edward and Lyndsy know how pleased he was with the android. Harold just hoped their boy would survive and get a chance to grow up. If Harold ever found Augustus, Harold knew he would do everything in his power to keep the boy safe from Phillipe. It was the least Harold could do for the boy's parents.

Chapter 2 D.I.Y.

He was alone for now. He had just gotten a new job to do. The money was good. About as good as he was. Douglas Ira Younon packed up his few meagre things and prepared himself for a new adventure. A client wanted him to hack into the Guardian Archives on the Edmunch Estate.

It didn't sound too hard of a job. He had learned there were some tours which anyone could go on to visit and learn more about the Edmunch Estate. He smiled to himself. He had been a hacker for most of his life. He would hack into computers he could get to physically. He would always leave his initials behind, which tended to baffle people for years.

He chuckled to himself. D.I.Y. was all people would find whenever they tried to find out what had happened to the computer files. No one had figured it out. He had no fears anyone ever would. But he was no longer the best hacker in the Universe anymore. As he well knew, that title now belonged to Melyssa Byte.

He finished packing his bag and left the hotel room. He had a bad habit of bouncing around and not always knowing where he would be sleeping at night. He was getting tired of that life. Yet, he still had memories of meeting people who were considered important. Such as Renée Rosendroff and her twin brother Phillipe.

He couldn't stop smiling. That night he spent with Renée was one he couldn't forget. He doubted he could keep up with her now. He chuckled remembering how hard it was to keep up with her then when he was young and inexperienced. Now it wouldn't matter. If she was still the same, he wouldn't come close to satisfying her.

He checked out of the hotel and left for the spaceport. He recalled there had been other wild nights with other women, but Renée was the best. He didn't deny it. He never knew that one night could change his life. He got to the spaceport and booked himself a ride to Nymphe. It was time to see if he was good enough to hack into the Guardian Archives.

He figured it would be easier to do it at a physical location of the archives rather than try remotely. It was also the way he typically worked. As he waited to board his spaceship, he went over what he knew about the Guardians. Many still considered them a myth even if they had any dealings with them. Some thought the Guardians weren't as prevalent as the rumours claimed.

He sat down and set his bag between his feet. He wasn't sure they were a myth. Too many things he had seen over the years made him wonder. He figured they had to be good at hiding or else everything would be known about them. Indeed, there were stories which couldn't be completely confirmed.

Douglas wondered if the Guardians were aware of him or at

least of his initials he left behind him at every job he'd ever done. If they were aware of him, why hadn't they tried to stop him or contact him in any way? He shook his head. There was no way of knowing for sure.

It could be they weren't interested in a hacker such as himself. He could readily believe they had their own hackers. But why not ask him to help out if they were into saving the scientists, inventors and others to hide them within their holds so they could do their lives' work?

He heard his boarding call. He stood up and grabbed his bag. Soon he was on the spaceship ready for takeoff. He got comfortable. He had a few days trip before he would be able to find the Edmunch Estate.

Chapter 3 Revenge or Learning

Phillipe Rosendroff stood in front of an android alcove as he frowned. He could see some obvious differences between it and an ordinary robot alcove. He sighed. Freedom snuck up behind him. She was naked and ready to play.

"Phillipe, do you have to work all the time?"

"What?" He turned around and smiled at her. "Well, I don't have to work right now." He grabbed her.

It didn't take them long to reach the bed and play for a bit. As he climaxed, his mind wandered again.

"Freedom, how can you be so good at this?"

"I had good teachers."

"No robot can do what you do."

"I know." She pinned him down. "Are you having trouble?"

"Not from you. I just can't figure out your alcove."

"Oh?"

"Yeah. I don't see how the Edmunch family could have surpassed me in that area."

She leaned over him. "Is that the whole trouble with you? You can't stand the Edmunch family because they understand androids?"

"Yes. I wish I could do just as well."

She laughed as she laid down on top of him. "That's too bad. You're such a genius with robots, that I can't see what you're missing."

They started another round of play.

"Robots are just machines and cold. You look like an elf and you are warm and inviting."

She laughed as she drew him close. "Perhaps that's your problem. You think robots are mere machines. Have you ever thought they could be people?"

"No. Robots? People? That's ridiculous."

"Is it? Am I a machine or a woman built for your pleasure?"

"You're a woman built for my pleasure!"

"Of course I am. I am a person. If you could think of robots as people, perhaps you could find the answer you seek."

"Oh! I don't know." He pushed her down on her back and climbed on top. "Robots aren't very smart. I've tried to program them to be pleasure robots, but they are too cold and clumsy. They fail where you excel."

"As I said, I had excellent teachers and I could practice with Pursuit."

"Then why are your alcoves different?"

"You might as well ask why I can sleep and eat as you do."

"Oh! There must be something in that." He took more plea-sure from her. "So, you have more complex brains than the robots. Is that it?"

"That's a big part of it."

"Do you know or you just playing with me?"

She laughed. "Do you care? I'm having a lot of fun with you."

"Do you know how to build an android?"

"No."

"Do you know how you work?"

"No."

He sighed. "Now, that's enough. I need answers."

She move her hands over his naked body. "I don't have the answers you seek, but I'm sure you can figure it out." Once more she got on top of him and gave him so much pleasure, he moaned.

"Oh! Fine. I'll do it without you." He relaxed and soon fell asleep.

She laid next to him with a big smile on her face. She didn't know everything about androids other than they were designed to be much like elves or other biological beings. She was content as she was and did her job well. So well that Phillipe never had time or energy to plan any revenge against the Edmunch family.

Chapter 4 The Guardian Archives

Clairis and Melyssa Byte were in the library checking the archives. Clairis was busy with maintenance and upgrades. As the librarian, she had to maintain the archives and keep the files from getting corrupted. It was routine work she never minded doing. She just knew it had to be done periodically so all the information would remain well preserved.

Mel was busy learning some new things she didn't know. With permission she had obtained, she could learn more than she ever had thought possible. She did learn about Aug and his inheritance and now she was learning something new that was too fascinating to her.

"Clairis, I see there are lots of unsolved hackings with D.I.Y. left behind. I think it's a calling card of a hacker."

Clairis smiled. "That's what we've thought for years. But we have never been able to find out who it is. Perhaps that hacker has a sense of humour?"

Mel chuckled. "Perhaps. Could it be someone's initials?"

The librarian shrugged her shoulders. "Doesn't it stand for do it yourself?"

Mel nodded. "Of course it does, but I'm not sure it isn't someone's initials."

"As I said, we don't know who it is, but there are numerous occurrences of those letters at different computers where files were stolen."

"So, why has it been so hard to find this particular person?"

"I'm not sure. I think every time it happened, people were stunned by the letters and thought the person was quite cocky."

"D.I.Y. was the greatest hacker in the universe, but anymore seems to be in decline. Could they be older and slowing down?"

Clairis smiled. "Now that's interesting. I hope you're not implying all old people slow down."

Mel smiled. "No, not in a mean way. People do tend to slow down when they get older. It's not a bad thing, I'm just wondering if that's what happened to this particular hacker."

"You took their place."

"Me? How did I do that?"

"You really don't know?"

Mel shook her head.

"You can do it remotely. D.I.Y. doesn't appear to have tried to hack any computer remotely. Every time, it was clear the hacker was in the same room with the computer."

"Oh, that's an interesting distinction."

"Yes, and usually hackers do it remotely and get caught that way. You could have lost your computer doing what you've done. But it doesn't always happen when accessing the specific computer in person rather than remotely."

Mel smiled. "Yes, it's tricky. My uncle taught me that when I was a kid. So, I learned how to bypass and not trigger such apps when I was hunting for information. I also didn't steal it. I left it and made copies for myself and my clients. Often sharing it online with the world."

"Yes, you are quite good with that. So, do you have an idea of how we could catch D.I.Y.?"

"Perhaps look for a pattern in which computers were hit."

"We've done that. We couldn't find anything at all."

"So, this hacker works for clients."

"Random clients with random assignments."

"Do you have security for the archives in case someone unauthorized comes in and tries to steal files?"

Clairis frowned. "Of course. You don't think D.I.Y. would try to hack into the Guardian Archives?"

"I think it possible. I'm sure the Guardians have enemies who don't want their information known to the universe."

"I see how you're coming up with this." Clairis blinked. "And we now offer tours."

"Yeah. What if D.I.Y. comes here?"

"They'd be caught, unless they are still good enough."

"I guess we need to keep an eye on anyone who comes on the tours."

"I'll tell Watson."

"I already did."

Clairis raised an eyebrow. "Oh, right you have a computer chip in your brain."

Mel smiled. "Yep. That's what I used. Watson already confirmed."

Clairis glanced back her computer. "He just gave me a message about it. He says he will keep a close eye on anyone who comes now." She paused to check the computer's progress. "I'm almost jealous. Sometimes I wish I had a computer chip in my brain."

Mel laughed. "You don't want one, especially if my uncle programs it. I would have to hack into it and reprogram it to something more suitable for you."

"Good point. I'll remain as I am, even if I am getting older and slowing down a bit."

Both ladies laughed.

Chapter 5 Tour

Douglas found himself on the Edmunch Estate. He was in a group of other tourists. Their tour guide was a robot. He listened intently and followed the robot around the estate. When they got to the library, Douglas found himself conflicted between going on with the tour and remaining in the library where he knew the Guardian Archives were.

He watched the tour guide and the other tourists. He blinked. He found an opening and didn't go on with the tour. He stepped back inside the library. He found a computer console and started doing his thing. He smiled. He remembered doing this hundreds of times before. The computers never had a chance against him.

Until now. Alarms blared and the computer console locked up. He gasped. He looked around him. He stood up and headed towards the door. The door slid open to reveal Watson with a couple of robots.

"Halt, sir."

Douglas gaped at Watson. "I don't know what happened. I got lost."

Watson raised an eyebrow. "Doubtful you got lost. You just didn't go on with the rest of the tour as you should have done."

Douglas shrugged. "So, now what?"

"Your name."

The computer scanned Douglas without any warning. The computer announced, "Douglas Ira Younon."

"Oh, are you the elusive D.I.Y. who stoled files from hundreds of computers?"

Douglas spread his hands palms outward. "In the flesh."

"Ah, then you must know you are no longer the greatest hacker alive."

Douglas sighed. "That title now belongs to Melyssa Byte."

Watson smiled. "She will be happy to know you are her biological father."

"What? How can that be?"

"Clearly you must have had sex with her mother."

"Well, of course, but I never knew I had a daughter. I thought I didn't have any children."

The library door slid open again and in walked Melyssa Byte. She stared Douglas down. She blinked.

Douglas' jaw dropped. She looked too much like Renée Rosendroff. "Uh, is this Melyssa Byte?"

"Yes, I am and you are the famous D.I.Y."

He nodded. "Is your mother Renée Rosendroff?"

She nodded.

"Oh, that explains it. I believe she got married not too long after that wild night we had."

Mel scoffed.

"I'm sorry. Would it help to know I could barely keep up with her even though I was quite young at the time?"

Mel rolled her eyes and looked at him. She chuckled. "You were definitely with my mother."

"Uh, am I under arrest?"

Mel smiled. "Not quite. You did try to hack into the Guardian Archives. There will be consequences. I suggest you tell the librarian everything she wants to know."

"Will I be able to leave the estate then?"

She shook her head. "No. You'll stay here. We'll give you a room of your own and someone will be looking after you to make sure you don't leave."

"Okay, so I'll be asked questions and then you'll decide what to do with me?"

"That's correct."

"So, where is the librarian?"

Mel shrugged her shoulders.

Watson said, "She's in her quarters taking a nap."

Mel said, "I know you have hacked hundreds of computers around the universe. You've got quite a reputation."

"But I'm no longer the greatest hacker in the universe. You surpassed me. I suppose I should take it as a compliment that you're my biological daughter."

She smiled. "I always wondered who you were and now I have a good idea. It figures that I could be a better hacker than my uncle ever was."

"Oh, did you start as a child?"

She nodded. "My uncle needed information and he couldn't get it on his own. He taught me what he knew and I surpassed him quite quickly. I'm not sure he liked it."

Douglas asked, "I hate to ask, but are your mother and uncle here?"

She shook her head. "No, they stay on the Rosendroff Estate. I don't usually see them unless they decide to drop in unannounced."

Watson sighed.

Douglas raised an eyebrow. "I suppose I shouldn't be surprised about that."

Mel asked, "If you only saw them once, then how could you know that?"

"I heard from others. I hear they can be quite ruthless and they probably had something to do with the murder of Edward and Lyndsy Edmunch."

"And I'm married to their son Augustus Edmunch."

Douglas gaped again. What had he gotten himself into now? He knew then it was his last hack job he would ever do. He would have to retire before he gotten into even more trouble.

Chapter 6 Breakthrough

"Oh!" Phillipe sat up in bed. "Finally." He stood up and walked over to the alcoves. "So, that's it! Now I see it!"

Freedom murmured and rolled over. She leaned on an elbow and smiled at him. "What do you see now?"

"I see how androids and robots are different."

"Oh, really."

"Yes, androids are far more complicated and similar to biological beings. Robots are just simple machines that represent more complex organisms. No wonder I couldn't get androids."

She sat up. "Did you figure it out completely?"

He nodded. "Now I need to design a whole line of pleasure androids. We can test them out and prepare them for their jobs in the universe."

She laughed. "Wonderful. Renée would love to help with the promotion part."

Renée and Pursuit entered the lab. They were just as naked as Phillipe and Freedom.

Renée blinked. "Working again, Phillipe?"

"Yes, I finally get it. Now I'm trying to design a line of pleasure androids we can test and train."

Renée smiled. "Sounds wonderful. Will they be as good as Pursuit and Freedom?"

Phillipe turned to face his sister. "Yes, of course. I understand it all now. It's really very simple. Now what do you want in your pleasure android?"

Renée swung her hips. "Well, I want one who can keep up with me and can do lots of different positions."

Pursuit said, "I do all that."

Renée smiled at Pursuit. "I know you do, but Phillipe is brainstorming. I know some of the pleasure androids will be for me and some for him. I will have to market them. He's not good at that part." She nodded. "Yes, I can promote this line of pleasure androids."

Phillipe smiled. "Of course you can do all the marketing. I trust your judgement on that. Now, let's get down to the specifics." He turned back to the alcoves and walked over to the computer console. Soon he was drawing up plans for new androids.

Renée laughed. "Yes, don't forget to make them look as beautiful and appealing as we are."

Phillipe smiled. "Of course I won't forget that. I'm just making sure I have the complex bodies down first. There, now I'm onto the skin and the shape."

Renée walked over to her twin. "Much better. I'm so glad you've figured it out."

"So am I. There. The designs are complete. The training will be a separate thing."

The robots in the lab began to build some androids. Renée

reached out for her brother. She smiled at him.

"Let's go to my room and celebrate your discovery."

They grabbed each other and made out as they stroked each other. Freedom stood up and walked over to Pursuit. They stroked and played too. No one made it to Renée's room and no one cared. They played and enjoyed themselves too well to care.

The days blurred for them after that. Between designing androids and training and testing them, no one had any thoughts of revenge. Instead they were happy designing their pleasure androids. It didn't take Renée long to come up with a marketing plan for them. Once a few models were ready for sale, she went right to work with filming commercials. Once the commercials were released, many people started to respond. It was clear that the androids were wanted and Renée was still quite attractive after all the time which had passed for her.

Chapter 7 Loss or Gain?

Douglas sighed as he sat on the bed. He was alone for now and wasn't sure of what was going to happen next. He just knew he was going to be grilled by the librarian. His door chimed. He blinked.

"Uh, you may come in even though I'm not fully dressed."

The door slid open and Tessa walked in. Douglas blinked. He thought she was beautiful and couldn't understand why she was sent to check on him.

"Do you require anything?"

He shrugged.

"Clairis the librarian is ready for you. I suggest you get dressed before seeing her."

"Oh, she doesn't want to see a half naked man?"

"Doubtful she does. I can step outside and wait until you're dressed."

He blinked. "Okay. Shouldn't take me too long."

Tessa bowed and stepped out into the hallway. The door slid shut behind her.

Douglass grabbed some clothes and got dressed. He sighed. He wasn't sure if he had lost something or had just gained something wondering. He shrugged and stepped out into the hallway. He smiled at Tessa. "So, how long have you worked here?"

"Not very long."

"Can you tell me anything about Clairis?"

"She has white hair and knows everything about the Guardian Archives."

"Oh. Is she the one responsible for the security?"

"Yes, on this estate and for the Guardian Archives she is."

"Is she mean or nice or somewhere in between?"

"I don't know what you mean by that. I haven't gotten on her bad side." She led the way back to the library.

"I just wanted to know what I would be in for with her questions."

"Just answer her honestly. She's looking for information. You are the famous D.I.Y. which no one has caught until now. She is quite interested in you and your clients. She wants to know your motives and how you work."

"Oh, then that doesn't sound too bad."

"Glad to hear to it."

"So, you do anything for fun?"

"Like what?"

"Oh, I don't know. Ever date anyone?"

She raised an eyebrow. "Are you asking me out on a date?"

"Well, if you're interested. How about dinner? Just the two of us? We could get to know each other better."

"Hmm. Depends upon what Clairis does with you." She stopped at the library. "You may go in now."

"Alright. I hope to see you later on."

Tessa smiled as he stepped inside the library. Douglas walked inside and saw a white haired lady sitting at a computer console. He approached her quietly.

"I suppose you are Clairis?"

"Sit down on the bed scanner, D.I.Y."

He did as she requested. She did something on her computer he couldn't see. Soon he was thoroughly scanned.

"Is this necessary?"

Clairis turned around to face him. "Yes, it is. Watson said the initial scan confirmed you are Melyssa Byte's biological father. I'm just doing a better scan to see if you are related to anyone else. It can also give us a better understanding about her."

"Oh. I thought you were going to ask me lots of questions about my work."

"I'm getting to that. Ms. Byte was the one who figured out D.I.Y. isn't just an acronym, it's also your initials and stands for Douglas Ira Younon. You've been quite elusive for much of your life."

He spread his hands out. "It seemed easy for me when I was younger. No one seemed to notice me."

"Hmm. Not hard to see why. You have an ability to blend in easier than others."

He lowered his hands. "The first time I hacked into a computer, I was just a teen and I was caught."

She raised an eyebrow.

"Then it got weird for me. Instead of being punished and thrown into jail, I was asked to hack his competitor's computer. I was offered money and freedom in exchange for the job. So, I accepted and did exactly what he wanted. I stole the files and left my initials behind."

"Really? Is that how it all started for you?"

"Yeah. Then I was given other jobs from that client and others. They tended to find me and I usually had plenty of work to keep me afloat. I started traveling and always remained with little luggage to hinder me. I've had a good run and was the best until Melyssa Byte came on the scene."

Clairis asked, "Does it bother you that she's surpassed you?"

"Well, I was intrigued at first. I was curious as to who she is. Now I know she's the result of the night I spent with Renée Rosendroff." He paused. "I never thought about settling down or having any children. So, I'm still not quite sure what to think about being a father. I'm just glad it was my own biological daughter who surpassed me."

"Oh? You can live with her as the greatest hacker in the universe?"

"Sure, why not? I think it's a compliment that a daughter I didn't know I sired by accident is a better hacker than I am. I would think it meant she got her talent from me."

Clairis smiled. "So, you want to get to know her better?"

"Yes. I see we have some important things in common. I take it she ran away from her mother and her uncle."

"Yes and she has her reasons which I can understand."

"Alright. I ran away too and I don't know what happened to my parents. Probably wasn't good and they might be relieved that I took off so young."

Clairis said, "So, there's something dark in your past."

"Yeah, a bit. I never knew my biological father and from what my mother told me about him, he sounded like bad news. Just played with her and left."

"You did the same thing."

"I know. However, I know Renée just wanted to play."

Clairis nodded. "She has quite a reputation in that area. I think you're correct about that part."

"Renée didn't tell me either. I don't know what happened between my parents, but my mother fell down into a deep depression. I got the impression that she felt I was a burden she didn't know how to get rid of. She did take care of me when I was very young, but she drifted away when I got older. Could I have reminded her of my father and what happened to her as a result?"

"It's possible. I don't know for sure and we don't have that in the archives. As for Renée, she may not have known who the biological father was. Just let everyone assume it was her husband's." She paused. "Sounds as if you did the right thing for you and saved yourself through the hacking."

He sighed. "I think it means something that I finally got caught. Perhaps I should just retire."

Clairis said, "I can't make that decision for you. What files were you looking for this time?"

"Files relating to the cyborgs and androids. I don't know what the client wanted specifically."

She frowned. "Cyborgs? Androids? Could it be some of our famous androids?"

He shrugged. "I have no idea. I take it they wanted all the files erased from the archives. That's all I know."

"Hmm. Interesting. We might be able to let you have some cyborg and android files to see what they are really after."

He blinked. "What?"

"I don't know who it is, but there's no reason why we can't let you have access to those particular files. However, they will remain a part of the archives."

"Of course. So, you want me to send them copies of those requested files?"

She nodded. "We can add a tracing app to follow them and what they are interested in. We need to know who this is and what they want."

"So, are cyborgs and androids real?"

"Of course they are. They just don't always come out of hiding anymore. They don't like to be treated badly. They don't like the prejudice."

"Can't say I blame them."

"Let me know when they contact you again. In the meantime, I will prepare the app and the files for you."

"So, that's it? I can just leave?"

"You can't leave the estate, but you may leave the library."

Douglas nodded and stood up. He left the library soon after just as confused as ever. He stepped into the hallway to find Tessa standing by the door. "You still here?"

She turned to him. "Yes. I see you survived."

"I guess so."

"You said you wanted dinner with me."

"Yes."

"Then let's have dinner. Follow me."

He smiled and followed her. She led him out to the garden where a little table for two was set. They sat down.

"So, what do you want to know, D.I.Y.?"

"Well, why are you working here of all places?"

"I like it here. I was offered the job right away and I do like everyone who lives and works on the estate."

"Does that include all the robots?"

She smiled. "Yes, it does. They aren't so bad once you get to know their little quirks. They tend to do most of the work on the estate. Without them, we'd be lost."

"I see. I haven't always been around robots and not sure of

all they can do, but I don't mind them." He paused to sample some food. "Ever think you'd want to be somewhere else?"

She shrugged. "I'm quite content here. There's a lot to learn."

"Really?"

"And it's getting interesting with you here."

He smiled. "Glad to hear it. I think you and Melyssa Byte will make my time here quite interesting. I just don't know if I'm supposed to be under arrest or if I'm allowed to be a guest."

"Perhaps we haven't decided that for you yet."

"Oh, now you're just playing with me."

"Would you like to meet Melyssa Byte's husband?"

"Sure."

"It will be arranged."

"Oh and will I be able to continue to see you?"

"Yes, that shouldn't be a problem."

"I won't be distracting you from your work?"

She shook her head. "No, I am currently assigned to keep an eye on you."

"So, you're my jailer. Hmm. Why did they have to pick someone so beautiful to keep me put?"

She laughed. "You're just making my job easier."

He smiled at her. Perhaps being stuck on the Edmunch Estate wasn't going to be so bad for him with Tessa around.

Chapter 8 Family News

Tessa led Douglas to the living room where Mel and Aug were lounging. There was a giant screen on the wall in front of them. Tessa showed Douglas where they could sit.

"This is Augustus Edmunch. Aug, this is D.I.Y. a.k.a Douglas Ira Younon."

Aug said, "Hello. I heard the news that you're Mel's biological father and you tried to hack into the Guardian Archives on my estate."

Douglas smiled. "Yes, I never knew about Melyssa until she surpassed me as a hacker. I am happy to learn she's my daughter. It certainly makes it easier for me to take it as a compliment that she surpassed me fairly early in her life."

Mel raised an eyebrow. "Really? You weren't upset about losing your title?"

"Well, I was shocked at first. Who wouldn't be? But it's much easier for me to take now that I know you must have gotten your talent from me."

Aug said, "Well, you two have that in common. Anything else?"

Mel said, "I think we both find robots and androids comforting."

Douglas frowned. "What are you talking about?"

Tessa laughed. "I'm an android. Didn't you know?"

Douglas gaped and blinked. "You are?"

Mel said, "Yeah, Aug and I tend to build androids based on his parents' work. She's just the latest."

Douglas sighed. "I see. You didn't make her just for me, did you?"

Mel laughed. "No. We didn't know you'd be here, but she's come in handy to keep an eye on you. I know we don't have to do any kind of lockdown to keep you on the estate."

Douglas smiled. "Okay, you got me. Tessa is beautiful and I'd like to get to know her better as long as she's okay with that."

Tessa said, "I'm okay with it."

Mel said, "Very good. It is always better to seek permission rather than forcing others into those sorts of relationships."

Douglas said, "I don't see where the fun is when you force someone. It's better when they want to too. If they're not interested, then it's best to walk away and leave them alone."

Tessa said, "Oh, good attitude. Ever had any serious relationships?"

"Sadly, I've been bouncing around for a long time. No time to start any. So, what about Melyssa and Augustus. How did you get together?"

Aug said, "We met on the last regular job we both had. I had to train her and then we became friends. Actually, we became best friends even though I knew I had other feelings for her. She made it clear she wasn't interested. She hated to be pursued and her attractiveness she inherited from her mother tends to make others jealous of her."

Mel said, "I wasn't looking for anything. I didn't even know his family was rival to mine. I had runaway and changed my name. It wasn't until I went digging for information for Aug that I learned who he was and then learned that my family was rivals to his. It was a shock to me, but we've never been rivals to each other."

Douglas smiled. "Sort of Romeo and Juliet without knowing about it at first."

Mel smiled. "Perhaps. My uncle kidnapped Aug and put a computer chip in his brain. I hacked into the chip and reprogrammed it so my uncle couldn't control him. Later, my uncle did the same thing to me. I had to hack into my chip and do the same thing. It really made my uncle mad."

Douglas laughed. "Yes, I recall your uncle couldn't handle someone being more of a genius than he was. So, you both have computer chips in your brains?"

Mel and Aug nodded.

"So, what does that mean? You have other abilities?"

Aug said, "We can talk to each other just using our chips. Something similar to telepathy, but using wireless technology."

Douglas said, "That must come in handy."

Mel said, "It certainly does. We can talk to the robots quickly and easily."

Douglas blinked. "You can talk to Tessa that way too."

Tessa said, "Yes, we can all do that."

On the screen appeared Pursuit and Freedom.

Mel said, "Oh and here are our two first androids we built to distract my mother and uncle from us."

"Hello, everyone. We have news that you'll love to hear about." Freedom smiled.

Pursuit said, "Phillipe Rosendroff has figured out how to create androids. He's busy creating a line of pleasure androids. Renée Rosendroff is marketing them. She tends to create videos with the androids to help explain what they can do."

Freedom said, "Phillipe is so happy now, he has no thoughts of revenge anymore."

Mel laughed. "Wonderful."

Aug laughed. "That's great. I'm not surprised about the pleasure androids. My parents were never into that."

Douglas asked, "You created androids to distract your mother and uncle?"

Mel nodded. "Yes. I figured they'd leave us alone with they had two androids who could keep up with them and keep them satisfied. It's worked out fairly well."

Aug said, "Until Phillipe found out they were androids. Then they all came here to complain. Except that Renée was quite happy with them. She convinced Phillipe to leave with the androids and leave us alone."

Douglas said, "Wow. That sounds like Renée. I barely could keep up with her before. I doubt I could now."

Mel frowned. "Why would you want to?"

He shrugged. "It was fun then, but it wouldn't be fun now. It doesn't even sound appealing."

Tessa said, "Looking for something else now?"

Douglas smiled. "Perhaps. I haven't decided yet."

Chapter 9 New Direction for D.I.Y.

Douglas was alone with Tessa in his room. He smiled at her.

"Tessa, do you like being and android?"

She shrugged. "I have no way of answering that. I feel fine as I am."

"Good enough." He paused. "I think I like my daughter better than Renée."

"Oh?"

"Yeah, Melyssa is much more down to Earth and I can relate to her."

"And no pressure to have sex with her?"

"That's disgusting. Why would you even ask that?"

"Well, you did say you had trouble keeping up with Renée and we all know Renée and Phillipe tend to have sex with each other."

"What? That's even worse…"

"That's why Mel left and changed her name. She was Lynda Rosendroff."

"Oh, I did hear about her. I guess it makes sense now. I know Renée got married after our night together and he was known to be Lynda's father."

Tessa nodded. "That's correct, but we know it's not true. DNA says something else."

He blinked. "I didn't hear much about Lynda other than her

existence. I don't think I ever saw her all grown up either. No wonder I didn't know she was mine biologically. I hope she's not mad at me for not being there for her."

"Mel hasn't complained about that. She was afraid her biological father was her uncle. She's actually relieved it's someone else and he was once the greatest hacker in the universe."

He smiled. "Good. That's something. Do you think she and her husband would mind me staying here? I would like to get to know her better."

"They won't mind a bit. You've been good so far."

"Oh, do they know about my decision already?"

She nodded.

"Well, okay. That makes that easier." He reached for her hand.

She took his hand.

"So, now that I'm staying, I think I would like a relationship. Are you willing?"

She smiled. "Will we be exclusive like Mel and Aug? Or do you want to play with others too?"

He raised an eyebrow. "Uh, I don't want to play with others like that anymore. I just want to settle down with one person. I also don't want to have to worry about having to try to satisfy someone like Renée."

She laughed. "Then I accept."

He smiled and kissed her on her cheek. "Are you one of the

pleasure androids Mel and Aug created?"

She shook her head. "I don't know about those things. Just Pursuit and Freedom had that training."

"So, what were you trained to do?"

"Be a personal assistant and perhaps back up to Watson."

"You're good at that." He paused. "Wait, is Watson an android?"

She nodded. "How did you guess?"

He shrugged. "I'm not sure. He seems to be fairly biological to me, but I guess there was something about his hair and skin not aging as Clairis' has."

Tessa laughed. "He offered to gray his hair to make her feel better, but she scoffed at him."

Douglas laughed. "I guess Mel is right. I do feel comfortable around robots and androids."

They kissed.

Chapter 10 Androids for Sale

Renée's campaign to sell the pleasure androids was working out for her and Phillipe. She appeared in short videos where she presented the various androids they had for sale. Her clothes were very revealing and she flirted dangerously with all of the androids. Of course the androids responded favorably to her. The results were excellent sales for the Rosendroffs.

Sometimes Phillipe would appear in the videos flirting with the androids too. He didn't wear much and didn't leave much to the imagination. Soon it was clear they would be quite financially solvent for years to come. Articles appears all over the internet and in newspapers and magazines about the Rosendroff pleasure androids.

Renée appeared on tv and on podcasts talking about the androids. Of course Mel and Aug followed and smiled at the success. It meant Mel and Aug could live in peace and not have to worry when Phillipe would be coming after them again. He was just too happy with the success of his pleasure androids to think anymore about revenge.

Even Douglas was happy. He had nothing to fear from anyone except the last client he had. He sighed when he received another message. This time he had to produce the files or be hunted. He walked to the library where he found Clairis. He sighed as he saw she was busy.

She looked up from her console. "What's the matter, Douglas?"

"My client has contacted me and requested the files asap."

"Very well. I see you have your tablet with you. That will help. Just one moment."

She faced her console again and interacted with the computer. His tablet beeped. He checked it and found a master file that the client had requested.

"Okay, I'll send it now." He sent the file and waited. He blinked. "I don't like this. Something seems a bit off with this last client."

"Oh? Ever had any trouble with clients before?"

"Not since the first one. They were pretty happy with my work and paid me well. This one is threatening me if I didn't send the files soon."

"Oh, I see. Could it be the first client you had?"

He shrugged. "I suppose it's possible. Hmm. Now that I think about it, I wouldn't be surprised if it was him."

She blinked. "We'll find out soon enough. The trace app is working."

His tablet beeped again. "They got it and they've sent me the money."

"I hope he paid you well."

"Yeah and I'm not doing any more hack jobs after this. I've had enough."

She smiled. "I heard you were staying here with us. Mel and Tessa are quite happy about it."

He smiled. "Good. I don't want to blow it. I would like to get to know my daughter better and enjoy Tessa. It's my first actual relationship. No more playing around for me."

"Good luck with that." She blinked. "We do have fairly good security here with all the robots. Some of use know how to fight as well. So, please don't worry if your last client comes here."

"I'll try not to. But if it's the same as my first client, it won't be pretty when he gets here."

"Probably not, but we should be fine."

He nodded to her and left the library with a nagging thought about his first client. Something he couldn't quite remember, but knew it had to be important. He shook his head. He had other things to do now. He looked forward to dinner with his daughter, her husband and Tessa. Then he would have some alone time with Tessa.

He smiled not knowing if he and everyone else living on the Edmunch Estate were in danger.

Chapter 11 Reactions to Androids

Renée and Phillipe Rosendroff's pleasure androids gained more popularity. Some were quite happy with their androids, while other started to complain about having androids as sex workers. The debates went on all throughout social media.

Some suggested androids should be created to be maids and personal assistants. Others went so far as to insist androids shouldn't replace biological beings. Renée and Phillipe were too busy with their androids to care about the debates. They continued to make more pleasure androids in different shapes and sizes. They were too focused on that market to venture out into anything else. They didn't want to and didn't think they needed to.

Mel smiled over the news and the debates. She set her tablet down and started to eat her breakfast. Aug was with her busy eating.

"Aug, perhaps it's time we started to release our own line of androids as maids and personal assistants."

Aug blinked. "Perhaps that is a good idea. I know the debates are heating up."

"We have a good start with Tessa and Watson. I'm sure some would be happier with androids rather than robots in their homes."

"There is that, but are you aware some people don't want androids to replace them?"

She blinked. "How would that work? Some people can't afford androids in their homes. We are more or less targeting the rich people with our line."

He nodded. "Perhaps you're right. I realize we have them here, but my parents already had money when they were discovering how to create androids."

"See. I grew up with robots because my uncle knew how to build them. They are already cheap and inexpensive labor. I honestly didn't know of any biological beings who still do housekeeping work. It seems too boring and menial for many people to try now."

"Some people have weird tastes and like to have biological beings for their maids."

"Um, I would think biological beings would be even more expensive than androids. Androids can just have alcoves. They don't have to eat as we do."

"Good point. Robots are even cheaper than androids, but still too expensive for many people to own."

"There are rental services people can use or even just to try out before they decide to buy. I know because that was how my uncle was able to keep the family afloat for years."

He glanced at her. "Did your mother ever earn any money?"

"Nope. She had no inclination at all in that direction. She just wanted to play all the time."

He chuckled. "I'm glad you like to work. I've never known you to be lazy."

She smiled. "Yeah, I'm not my mother."

"I think you have more in common with your father."

"I think so. Or at least from what I know of him so far."

"At least he's not causing any trouble."

"I think he really likes Tessa."

He smiled and chuckled. "Yeah, and we didn't create her to be a pleasure android."

"No, but she is happy with him. She told me she had to ask if he just wanted to be with her or play with others too and he told her he just wanted to settle down."

"Good. He did say he never had a chance to do that before. Always bouncing around and never staying with anyone."

"Well, I'm glad he didn't stay with my mother. He would have been miserable."

"Is your mother that bad?"

"Yeah, her husband couldn't keep up with her. He got old and died. I know she and my uncle tended to play with each other quite often because he was the only biological male who could keep up with her."

He sighed. "Mel, I know that incest bothers you."

"It still does, but I can accept it better when they leave me alone. They are doing that. My mother almost thanked me for the androids. That's more than I ever had from her before."

"Yeah, I remember that. She was the one who convinced Phillipe to leave. She wanted to keep the androids even though she knew they were spying on her and her brother."

"She has her priorities. Her pleasure is high on the list."

"And now your uncle is so happy with their line of pleasure androids that he doesn't care for revenge anymore."

"So, my plan worked. I gave them what they wanted which was the best way to keep them away from me. I already feel safer now. They are happy and don't mind that I'm not with them anymore."

"I still don't understand it all, but I can see how you thought it would work. It has worked and I'm glad. I don't want to live in fear that my in laws want to kill me and my wife."

She smiled and held his hand. "Yes, exactly. It is better this way. They leave us alone and we can leave them alone. I don't think they are harming anyone with their pleasure androids. If anything, the world can see how they are and make their own decisions."

He smiled and squeezed her hand briefly. "Yes, I know. I hope it continues."

Chapter 12 New Family

Aug, Mel, Tessa and Douglas sat around the dinner table. Watson stood nearby. They were enjoying their food and being with each other.

Mel said, "I see my mother and uncle are quite happy with their line of pleasure androids."

Aug said, "Yeah, they copied our design. Perhaps I should sue them."

Mel laughed. "No, they have their own designs. Haven't you noticed?"

Aug smiled. "Right. They don't have the instructors we found for our two pleasure androids."

Douglas smiled. "I've noticed too. I don't think I've ever seen either that happy before."

Everyone laughed.

Mel said, "I'm glad I came up with the idea. It's the gift that keeps on giving to them and to us."

Douglas blinked. "I take it, you didn't just want to give them a gift. You did it so they would be distracted from you."

Mel nodded. "Yeah and it worked. My uncle wasn't happy about it at first, but my mother was able to convince him it was better to accept the androids and leave us alone."

Douglas smiled. "And now Phillipe understands androids enough to create a pleasure line of them in different shapes and sizes. I'm not surprised that's all he's focused on."

Tessa said, "And yet people are asking for other kinds of androids to do menial labor and even be personal assistants."

Mel said, "That's where Aug and I come in. We can provide that kind of android for those who would rather have an android which looks like them rather than a robot that looks more like a machine."

Douglas raised his glass. "Well, I can drink to that. I'm glad the revenge has died in such a funny way and we are all better for it."

Everyone raised their glasses and accept the toast. They drank.

Watson cleared his throat. "I hate to interrupt, but I think we have a visitor. He appears hostile."

Everyone stopped the merriment.

Aug asked, "What do we need to do?"

Watson blinked. "The robots are meeting them." He paused. "Oh, he is here to see D.I.Y. and Melyssa Byte." He blinked again. "His name is Harold Rosendroff."

No one moved. Mel blinked. Aug blinked. Tessa twitched. Douglas gasped.

Mel said, "I didn't know there was a Rosendroff named Harold."

Douglas said, "He owned the first computer I hacked into and got caught. Why is he here now?"

Mel and Douglas met eyes and gritted their teeth.

Aug asked, "Have the Rosendroff family always been into robots and computers?"

Mel and Douglas answered at the same time through clenched teeth. "Yes."

Aug nodded. "Watson, let him in and contact both Renée and Phillipe. We may need their input for this."

Watson nodded. "I think it will be better if we go to the living room where the screen is large enough."

Everyone left the table to go to the living room as suggested. Moments later robots escorted Harold Rosendroff into the room. He walked slowly with a cane and sat down as soon as he could. He wheezed and coughed. He looked quite old with a few white wisps of hair and lots of liver spots on his head, face and hands.

Mel blinked. "I'm sorry, I didn't know there were other Rosendroff family members other than Renée, Phillipe and George."

Harold frowned. "I knew them well when I was young and spry as you are. I tried for Renée's hand and she rejected me." He slammed his fist down on the arm of the chair. "I can't believe that slut would say no to me. I was young for a Rosendroff and rich. No, she had to marry cousin George instead."

Mel raised an eyebrow. "I'm sorry, that is before my time."

"Clearly. If I didn't know any better I'd think you were Lynda

Rosendroff."

"I was. I changed my name to Melyssa Byte."

"Yes, I've heard of you. The best hacker in the Rosendroff family. No one could surpass you, except if you had a child of your own."

Mel shrugged. "Remains to be seen."

Harold frowned and stared at Douglas. "And you, D.I.Y. I remember when you hacked into my computer when you were just a teen. You were good even then, but I just happen to catch you. Did you get caught this time?"

Douglas nodded. "Security is just too good with the Guardian Archives."

Harold nodded. "Well, you gave me the files with a tracing app to it. I thought it best to come here and find what the hell is going on with the Edmunch Estate and the current owners."

Aug raised an eyebrow. "You didn't happen to know my parents, did you?"

"Ah, are you the son of Edward and Lyndsy Edmunch? I think I can see some resemblance."

Aug nodded.

"Well, you were hidden quite well for much of your life. Only the Guardians could be so sneaky as to hide you right under Phillipe's nose. He could be rather dense at times. So full of prejudice."

Clairis entered the living room and stood next to Watson.

Harold frowned at her. "Who the hell are you?"

Clairis frowned. "I could ask the same of you, but Watson already informed me. I am Clairis. I'm the Guardian Librarian."

Harold studied her. "Did you write the tracing app?"

She nodded.

"Impressive and clearly you're not as young as the current owners of this estate."

Clairis raised an eyebrow. "Is that why you came? To see who wrote the app?"

Harold nodded. "Partly. That and to see D.I.Y. once more and to meet Melyssa Byte who surpassed him as the greatest hacker in the universe. I should tell you it was D.I.Y. who surpassed me when just a boy."

Douglas raised an eyebrow. "Is that why you agreed to let me go if I did a job for you?"

"Yes. Also I was jealous and quite upset at first."

Douglas nodded. "I remember that."

"But then I realized you had the talent I needed. So, I used you in exchange to not press charges." He sighed. "I used your services over the years to keep tabs on my cousins Renée and Phillipe. I'm sure that's part of the reason why what your clients wanted was so varied and random."

Douglas blinked. "I know the Guardians wondered about that. I didn't really question it as I had good paying gigs to keep me afloat."

"Well, I had you erase the files and send them to me. I didn't want Phillipe to learn how to create androids and yet he has now. Who's responsible for that?"

Mel raised an eyebrow. "Well, Aug and I created two pleasure androids to keep Renée and Phillipe distracted from us. Phillipe was quite mad at first, but Renée was so happy with the androids that she was able to convince Phillipe to leave us alone. She accepted the bribe."

Harold laughed. "You are one of us in a way. You are smart enough and perhaps not quite as inbred as the rest of us."

Mel cringed.

"But you are better than we are in many ways. You're definitely stronger. You did what the rest of us couldn't. You walked away when you needed to."

Mel gaped. "I don't understand. Why was it so hard for the rest of you?"

Harold sighed. "It was the money and we didn't know how to survive without it. I at least could work and run a business. Renée hasn't done anything but play and now she's working for once in her life. Phillipe could build robots and I knew he was smart enough to learn androids eventually, but I kept thwarting him along the way. George didn't have a clue about work. He was raised to play.

"So, it's good to know there might be some hope for the Rosendroff legacy to survive even if I don't have much longer to live."

Mel asked, "What legacy? What are you talking about?"

"I'm an old man and was taught to respect the long family line with ties to nobility and such. I knew we had too much inbreeding to the point that we were in danger of disappearing. Now I know we won't. I was the one who put D.I.Y. in Renée's way."

Douglas gaped. "So, you planned Mel's birth?"

"In a way. I figured you wouldn't be able to resist her. And you didn't. I was suspicious when she had a baby after she hadn't been married that long to George. I asked him about it and he always knew Lynda wasn't his, but he never publicly denied it. He thought it best not to say anything."

Mel asked, "So, you expect big things of me?"

Harold smiled.

Chapter 13 Family Legacy Restored

Watson said, "I have finally reached Renée and Phillipe Rosendroff."

Renée and Phillipe appeared on screen with Pursuit and Freedom behind them. Renée looked at everyone on the Edmunch Estate and frowned when she saw Harold.

"Harold, I thought you were dead! You were such an old man when you dared to come after me."

Harold smiled. "Hello, cousins. I see you haven't changed. When you look at me, you could be seeing your own futures."

Renée and Phillipe scoffed at that remark.

Harold continued, "I'm glad we can have this little family reunion now." He coughed and wheezed. "As you can probably guess, I am dying. I don't have much time left."

Phillipe said, "Why are you telling us? We don't care if you die."

Harold smiled. "You should care. Is our family legacy worthless to you?"

Phillipe frowned. "What legacy?"

Harold continued, "I realize we are inbred due to incest, but it's more than that. We descended from the first elves who created computers and robots. Why else would you be so into building robots and androids?"

Phillipe gaped. "Can it be that our ancestors were a part of that?"

Harold nodded. "Our family goes way back. But we always had our jealousies and rivalries. We thought we were better, but slowly we were degrading the family line." He coughed. "When I realized the truth, I thought it best to try and save it as best I could. When I met D.I.Y. when he was a teen, I knew I had found an answer to the problem."

Phillipe said, "But you hated that kid from the start. You were jealous because he was a better hacker than you were."

Harold smiled. "That is true, but you always knew I was better at hacking than you were. I know you taught Lynda and she was better than both of us combined for a very good reason. D.I.Y. is her biological father."

Renée gasped. "I do remember him. He wasn't too bad. He was better than George. Would you like another round, Douglas?"

Douglas frowned. "No, Renée. I can't keep up with you now. I've grown older and I've settled down. I'm not cheating on her to try and make you happy."

Renée gasped. "How can you say no to me? I'm irresistible."

Harold laughed. "I think he grew up and knows what he wants now. Now you know how it feels for me when you rejected me."

Mel rolled her eyes. "So, Harold put Douglas in Renée's path to help insure one of us wouldn't be so inbred and could keep the family line going."

Renée and Phillipe gasped.

Harold smiled. "Yes, as head of the family, I felt I had to do something. Now you know why she's the greatest hacker in the universe now. Renée had some talent, but never really used it. Combine that with D.I.Y. and here we have one of us who isn't as inbred and could do what the rest of us aren't that good at anymore."

Phillipe sighed. "You are better at revenge than I ever was."

Harold said, "I play the long game. Sometimes it's better not to get back at people right away. Sometimes the universe takes care of them."

Mel asked, "So, this is what I inherit? A legacy of computer programmers and hackers and robot and android builders?"

Harold nodded. "Yes, and I'm not surprised Phillipe turned Augustus and yourself into cyborgs. I had heard some rumours and now I know it's true. I was afraid he might do such a thing and thought he should be stopped. But you surprised me, Melyssa Byte. You were able to hack into both chips and save yourselves. You have exceeded my expectations and hopes."

Mel smiled. "Well, now I know how it was possible, but I feel I need to bring up the fact that I also pushed myself to be better."

Harold nodded. "Determination counts for a lot."

Phillipe said, "So, is that all of the legacy?"

Harold smiled. "Well, there is some money and material wealth involved too."

Phillipe and Renée both sighed.

Phillipe asked, "Did you fund Edward and Lyndsy Edmunch's research?"

Harold answered, "Yes and I don't regret it. As you can see, the child I hoped that would surpass us all has married their son. So, things have worked out well for both families."

Phillipe face palmed himself. Renée frowned.

Renée sighed and asked, "What of the material wealth? Are we getting that?"

Harold shook his head. "I'm giving it all to Melyssa Byte to do with as she sees fit. Augustus will probably have a hand in that too and that's fine."

Renée frowned. "Very well, but at least we have our pleasure androids."

Phillipe nodded. "Yeah, we're a team and people are happy with our androids."

Harold smiled. "I'm glad you have that. I'm sure you two will be fine as far as money goes."

Mel asked, "So, would you care if we donated to charity?"

Harold shook his head. "Not at all. I'm sure you'll find something good to do with the money. Perhaps expose a few more criminals and sociopaths." He smiled.

Mel and Aug smiled. Mel was glad she wasn't exactly like her family and could just be herself and help those who needed it more than she did. Aug was happy to hear how his parents too had help when they were younger knowing it was impossible to get anywhere without the cooperation of others.

www.ingramcontent.com/pod-product-compliance
Lightning Source LLC
Chambersburg PA
CBHW052126150726
48002CB00006B/2494